Buzzy B..
"BEE HAPPY"

By Barbara Curie
Illustrated by Vera Gohman

ISBN: 0-87239-355-0

STANDARD PUBLISHING

Cincinnati, Ohio   3625

If you want to be happy . . .

This little book is just for you. The stories will help you know what to do. Read from your Bible and then obey; be cheerful and helpful as you go on your way. Make others happy and smile a big smile; then you will be happier all of the while.

Buzzy

VKG

Be Kind

There's a story I'd like to tell you, about Jamie Jones and his sister Sue. He teased her and teased her all the day long, even though Mother said it was wrong. Then one day at Sunday school, Jamie learned the golden rule. From that day on Jamie practiced on Sue, "Do unto others as you'd have them do unto you." And if Jamie forgot and teased Sue again, she would forgive him and they would be friends.

Jamie obeyed God and so did Sue. Read Ephesians 4:32.

Be Polite

The nicest boy I've ever known was Timothy Tyler Knight. Everyone always said of him, "Timothy is polite." He didn't just say, "Pass me the bread," or "Someone pass the peas." He said it in a special way; he always added "please."

He bumped into a man out on the walk one day; he stopped and said, "Excuse me, Sir," before he went his way. When people did nice things for him, or gave him something new, he always smiled his nicest smile and then he said, "Thank you."

The happiest boy I've ever known was Timothy Tyler Knight. Everyone liked to be his friend because he was polite. (Read Luke 6:31.)

dime, and it started to worry her after a time. She was very unhappy, as I think you would be, till she told all the truth and added, "Forgive me."

Obey God's Word if you want to be blessed; the Bible says, "Do that which is honest."

(Can you find those words in 2 Corinthians 13:7?)

Be Patient

Melissa Jane and her brother, Don, got a book in the mail from Uncle John. Don was first to look at the book. And Melissa got madder the longer it took. She even shouted at her older brother. Then she pouted until stopped by Mother. "You must wait and not complain. Learn to be patient, Melissa Jane."

Be Forgiving

Be a Friend

Leah went to the park at the end of the street. She saw a girl with crippled feet. Leah felt sad as she played games and ran. She thought, "That girl can't run and play like I can." Leah found where she lived and that her name was Elaine. Leah went to visit and took her favorite game. She said, "I'm Leah. I live in this block at the other end. I would like for you to be my friend."

Elaine was so glad to see Leah that day. She loved the game Leah brought to play. They found many things they both liked to do—work puzzles, play games, go to Sunday school, too.

Be a friend; You'll find it's fun. Read in the Bible 1 John 4:21.

Be Diligent

David grabbed his ball glove and out he ran. He was going to play catch with his neighbor, Dan. But his father called out, "Wait, David, come back. You made a promise to help Mr. Mack. You start on a project, then off you dart. You must learn to finish what you start. Learn to be diligent all your life through; that means to keep at it, whatever you do."

David decided that his father was right, and began to change that very night.

Days later he heard Mr. Mack say to his dad, "David's a good worker; you can count on that lad."

It's important to be diligent, and this can be seen by reading 2 Peter 3:14.

Be Faithful

Tina loved to go to Sunday school and stay for worship, too. She loved hearing Bible stories and learning each thing new. One Sunday morning, just before worship was to begin, Tina heard her name called out by Superintendent Jim. He pinned on her dress a pin of gold and red. "For perfect attendance" is what he said.

Tina felt happy and proud of her pin. She couldn't keep from showing her grin. Deep inside Tina felt good, because she was faithful and did as she should.

We are servants of God; it's His will that we do. Read 1 Corinthians—chapter 4, verse 2.